BALU Series
THE PAW-TRAVELER
Visits the Seven Modern Wonders

written by **Miry Bejerano**

illustrated by **Pavani Apsara**

THIS BOOK BELONGS TO

_____

Author's Note

To all the curious explorers and their families,

Traveling and discovering new places with the people I love has always been my passion. It's what inspired me to write this book.
My goal is to spark curiosity and encourage young readers to explore our incredible world.
While this is a work of fiction, all facts about the wonders are accurate, so readers can learn while diving into the adventure.

Enjoy the journey, and always remember to smile along the way.

Miry

Hello there! I'm Balu the Paw-Traveler. I'm so happy you're here to join me on this incredible adventure. Have you ever taken a trip on an **imaginary** airplane? I'll explain in just a bit. But first, let me tell you where we're going. I'm so excited!

We're going to explore the Seven Modern Wonders of the World! Have you heard of them? They're **amazing** places built long ago, and they still look impressive today. I've called friends at each Wonder, and they're ready to reveal some cool facts about every landmark! They can't wait to welcome us and even teach us some words in their native language. That will make our journey even more fun.

And guess what? When we return, I have a **surprise** for you! You're going to love it!

Now, let's get back to the imaginary airplane. It's a magical plane that you can create with your imagination!

It doesn't need wings or engines. Just close your eyes, picture yourself soaring through the skies, and you're already flying. You can go anywhere you want, from the tallest mountains to the deepest jungles, and never have to leave your seat. **Traveling** from one place to another is as quick as turning the page! We'll also try imaginary trains and hot air balloons. It's going to be so much fun. So, are you ready to travel with me? Here we go!

Close your eyes, take a deep breath... Now say this out loud:

"Adventure awaits, let's go!"

Feel the wind on your face and butterflies in your tummy as we take off into the sky. Whoosh! We're soaring through the clouds and ready for our adventure!

Balu's Notes

Hola!

This is the flag of Mexico.

We are here!

They speak Spanish.

Mexican Hat

Welcome to Chichen Itza, an ancient and fascinating city built by the Maya. Look at these huge stone structures! The one behind us is called *The Castle*, or *El Castillo* in Spanish. Cool name, right? I've explored these ruins many times, but I also love coming here for the delicious food! Have you ever tried tacos? They're little folded tortillas filled with tasty ingredients like meat, cheese, or veggies.

Just thinking about it made me hungry. **Yum!**
You should come back sometime and stay longer. I'd love to show you all the secret spots. We could even have a taco party by El Castillo!
Doesn't that sound fun?

Taco

That sounds **awesome!** We'd love to explore more and enjoy those tacos with you. But for now, let's keep this adventure in our minds and come back another day. Thank you Jaguar! It's time for us to head off to our next two destinations in South America.

Let's go discover!

MACHU PICCHU
PERU

Balu's Notes

Hola!

This is the flag of Peru.

We are here!

They speak Spanish.

Poncho

We're lucky today because the sun is shining, and we can see the entire **beauty** of Machu Picchu. This hidden city was built by the Incas long ago. It's high up in the mountains of Peru, surrounded by breathtaking sights. You'll see stone houses, twisty paths, and views that may leave you speechless!

I know you need to leave, but don't worry, I'll be here waiting! When you come back someday, keep an eye out for me.

I'd love to take some pictures with **friends** like you! Imagine us posing with the stunning mountains behind us. I'd be so glad to share this amazing adventure together!

Ceviche

Pan Flute

Yes, that would be **unforgettable**! Thank you for showing us around. See you again soon!

Alright, everyone, let's hop on my imaginary train! This train doesn't need tracks or fuel. Just close your eyes and picture it chugging along.

All aboard... Choo, choo!

Adventure awaits, let's go!

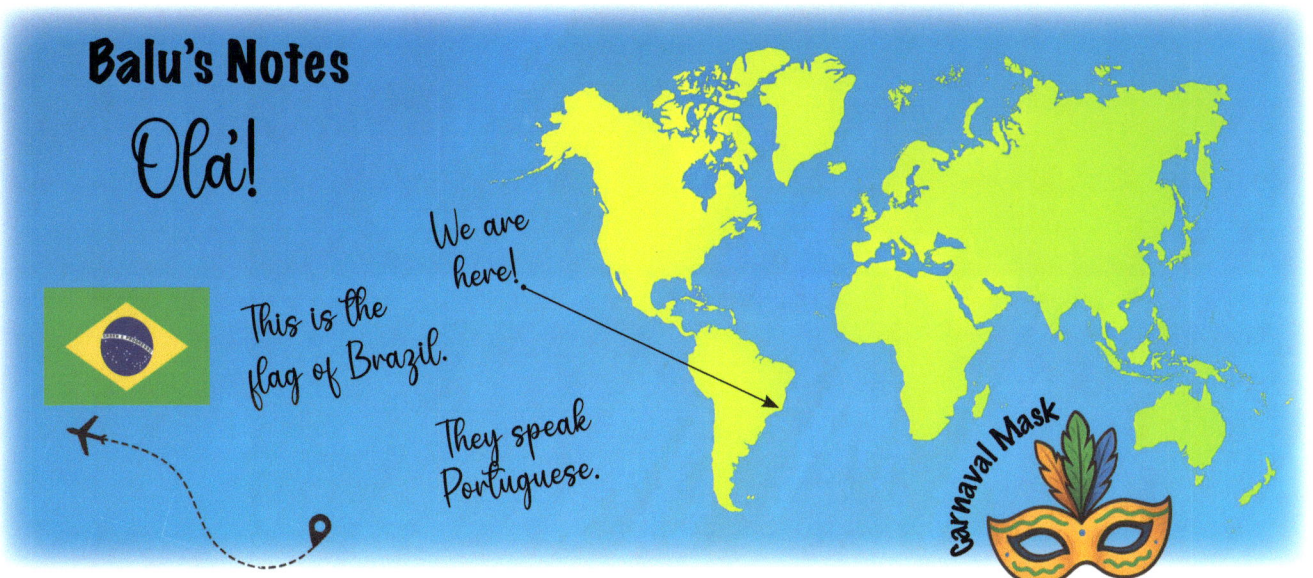

Balu's Notes

Olá!

This is the flag of Brazil.

We are here!

They speak Portuguese.

Carnaval Mask

Hello from Rio de Janeiro, my friends! Christ the Redeemer is an enormous statue of Jesus with open arms, standing proudly at the top of a mountain. But it's more than just a statue, it's a symbol of **love** and peace for everyone who visits.

Now that you've seen this fabulous sight, are you ready to learn some **samba** steps? Here's how:
- Step to the right, slide your feet together.
- Step to the left, slide your feet together again.
- Now add a little bounce, move your hips, and keep going.

Practice, practice, practice! You will be dancing like a pro in no time!

Picanha

Those steps are fun but a little tricky, so let's save samba practice for later. Obrigado! Now we're heading to another continent to explore the Colosseum in Rome.
Let's cross the Atlantic Ocean.
Off we go!

Balu's Notes

Ciao!

This is the flag of Italy.

We are here!

They speak Italian.

Vespa

My friends, welcome to Rome, the capital of Italy! Before I tell you about the Colosseum, here's an interesting fact. Did you know that the smallest country in the world is right here in the center of Rome? It's called *Vatican City*.

Pretty cool, huh?

Now, let me show you something epic. It's the Colosseum! Just look at it! It's a big circular building, shaped almost like a giant ring. In the past, huge crowds gathered here to watch exciting events, like gladiator games. Today, visitors from around the world come to explore these ancient ruins and imagine what life was like back then.

In Italy, we say 'Ciao!' to greet someone and also to say goodbye.

So ciao for now! I'm off to explore more of this **wonderful** city.

Gelato

Pizza

In that case, ciao, Pigeon!

Thank you so much for exploring with us. Now, my friends, get ready. We are heading to the biggest continent in the world: *Asia*. **It's go time!**

Balu's Notes

Marhaban!

This is the flag of Jordan.

They speak Arabic.

We are here!

Flat Bread and Hummus

I'm so **glad** you came to visit me! Petra is a unique city carved into the mountains, full of stunning temples and ancient houses. Long ago, the Nabateans made Petra their home.

There's so much to explore in this historic land, and I'm always here to guide you through this wonder. Oh, and if you're hungry, you've got to try the delicious traditional food! How about warm, fluffy flatbread, sweet dates, and creamy hummus? It's the **perfect** treat after a day of adventure.

So, what do you say?

Come taste the flavors of Petra with me!

Dates

That sounds very tempting. The food looks **delicious!** But we have to go, our hot air balloon is ready to take us to our next stop. Thank you, Camel! Okay friends, we don't need ropes or burners. Just close your eyes and feel yourself rising higher and higher. Can you feel the breeze?

Adventure awaits. Let's go!

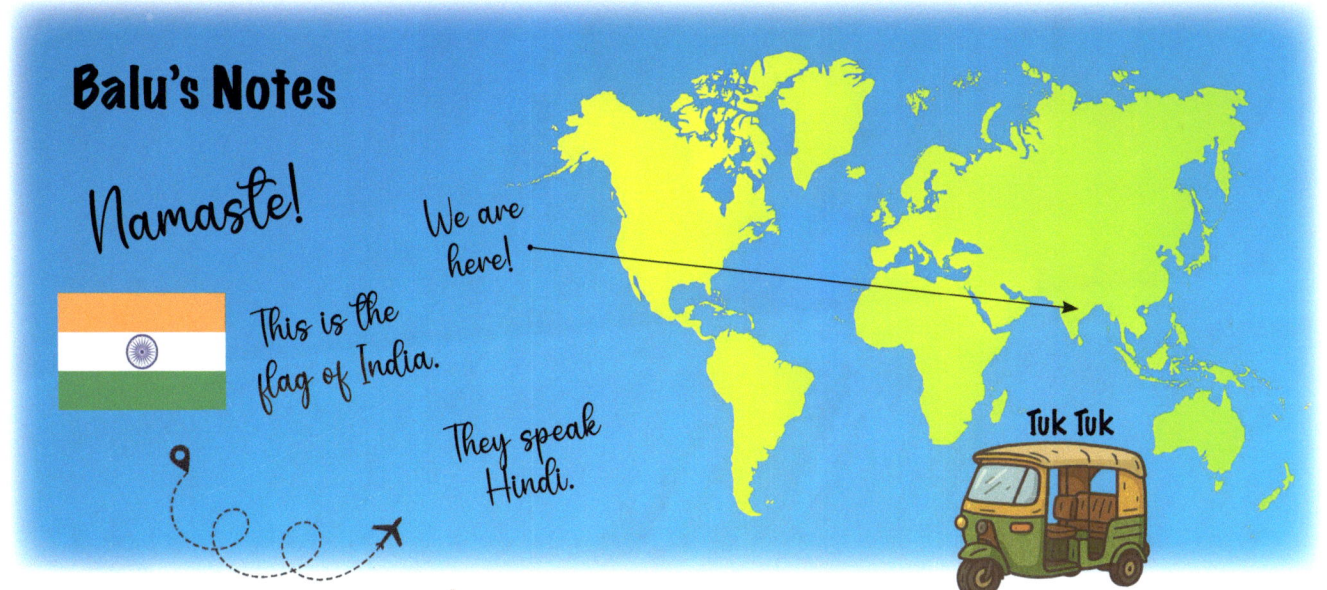

Balu's Notes

Namaste!

This is the flag of India.

We are here!

They speak Hindi.

Tuk Tuk

Wow, look at this shiny white building! We're at the Taj Mahal in Agra, India. Can you believe a king built this palace for his wife to show his **love**? It took 22 years to finish!
The big dome on top looks like a huge onion, doesn't it?
I was doing yoga in the garden before you got here. Yoga helps us feel **strong** and focused by moving our bodies and calming our minds. My favorite pose is the Tiger Stretch! Are you up for a challenge? Get on your hands and knees, lift one leg back like a tiger waking up from a nap, and let out a soft growl. Feels **good**, huh?

Gulal

Yeah, very **nice!** Thank you for sharing everything with us. We've learned so much from you. But it's time to say goodbye, just for now, as we head to our next adventure!
Let's get going!

THE GREAT WALL
CHINA

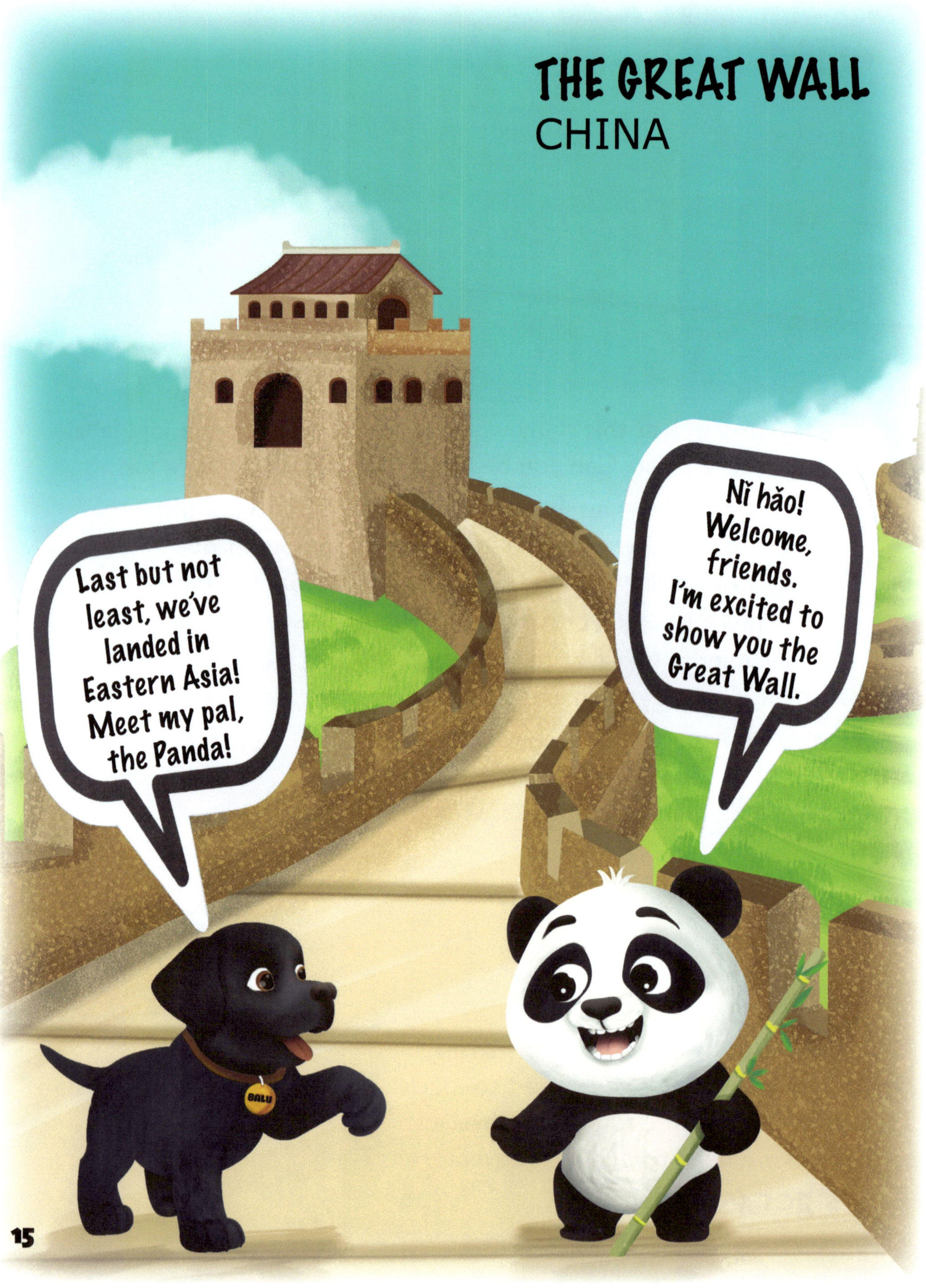

Balu's Notes

Nĭ Haŏ!

We are here!

This is the flag of China.

They speak Chinese.

Chinese Dragon

The Great Wall is like an endless snake made of bricks and stones, winding over mountains and valleys.

It was built a long time ago by the first emperor to **protect** the land. Now, it's like a big, sleeping dragon. Probably dreaming of dumplings.

Anyways, I'm about to practice some bamboo-stick kung fu! Want to try with me?

Grab your imaginary bamboo stick, stand tall like a warrior, and let out a big swoosh as you shout HIYA! Feel your arms getting **strong** and your body standing steady. Imagine guarding a wall as mighty as this one. Awesome, right? Maybe one day you'll come back and show off some new moves!

Chinese Dumplings

Wow, that was wild! Thank you so much, Panda, for teaching us those fun moves. I'm so glad we could explore this place **together**.
But now, it's time to start heading home, my friends. Let's get ready for our journey back.

Wheels up, travelers!

Wow, what an **adventure** we've had!

We explored the Seven Wonders of the World, learned fascinating facts about each one, and even picked up some words in different languages from our knowledgeable friends.

We've seen some of the most **extraordinary** places on Earth!

But our fun doesn't end here. Remember that **surprise** I promised?

Now, I've got two exciting activities for you to enjoy with your family and friends!

You'll find these activities on the next pages.
They'll bring back all the **excitement** and might even inspire you to explore more of these spectacular wonders.
Thank you so much for joining me! You've been an awesome travel buddy.
Until our next adventure, keep exploring, keep learning, and most importantly, **keep smiling!**

See you soon!

Balu's Family Game
Seven Wonders Challenge

Goal

Try to answer as many questions as you can. The player with the most correct answers wins!

What You Need

• This book.
• The list of questions on page 21 and 22.
• A piece of paper to write everyone's names.
• A pen or pencil.
• Small papers with numbers 1 to 30.
• A bowl to hold the papers.

Set Up the Game

• Write everyone's names on the paper.
• Make sure the book is nearby so you can look things up.
• Put the number papers in the bowl.
• Each player picks a number from the bowl. No peeking!
That number tells you which question to answer.

How to Play

Choose one person to be the game host. The host will read the questions out loud.
Everyone else takes turns answering the question that matches the number they picked.

Need help? You can look in the book!
If you get the answer right, you get a point.
If you're not sure, the host can ask the next player or give the answer. You get to decide how to play!

Who Wins?

The player with the most correct answers.

Helpful Tips

• Think before you answer.
• Use the book to help you.

Fun Twist

Try using a timer to make it more exciting.
If you have a big group, play in teams!

Enjoy the game!
The more you play, the more you learn.
Have fun exploring together!

Questions

1. Who greets us at the Taj Mahal in India?

2. What yummy food does Jaguar love to eat?

3. How do you get the imaginary airplane ready for takeoff?

4. What is the name of the statue we see in Rio de Janeiro?

5. What fun activity does Panda teach us at the Great Wall?

6. What tasty foods does Camel suggest trying in Petra?

7. Who greets us at the Great Wall of China?

8. What exciting events happened inside the Colosseum long ago?

9. What phrase does Balu say before starting the adventure?

10. What pose does Tiger show us to try in the garden of the Taj Mahal?

11. What does the big dome on top of the Taj Mahal remind you of?

12. What is the name of the smallest country located inside Rome?

13. Who do we meet at Chichen Itza in Mexico?

14. What does Christ the Redeemer's open arms symbolize?

15. What animal friend shows us around Machu Picchu?

16. What surprise does Balu promise?

17. What does the Toucan want to teach us in Brazil?

18. What is Petra carved into?

19. What does Panda say the Great Wall looks like?

20. Which wonder was built to protect the land?

21. What country is Machu Picchu located in?

22. Who shows us the Colosseum in Rome?

23. What did Balu ride that travels on tracks?

24. What else did Balu fly in besides a plane?

25. What is the name of the big pyramid at Chichen Itza?

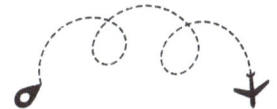

26. What did Llama say you can do when you visit Machu Picchu again?

27. How many years did it take to build the Taj Mahal?

28. How do you say hello and bye in Italian?

29. What was the Tiger practicing?

30. How many wonders did Balu take us to explore?

Use this code to find a video on how to play. Check out the Creative Corner.

1. Tiger (p.14), 2. Tacos (p.4), 3. With your imagination (p.2), 4. Christ the Redeemer (p.8), 5. Bamboo Stick Kung Fu (p.16), 6. Flatbread, dates, hummus (p.16), 7. Panda (p.16), 8. Gladiator's games (p.10), 9. Adventure awaits, let's go (p.2), 10. Tiger Stretch (p.14), 11. An onion (p.14), 12. Vatican City (p.10), 13. Jaguar (p.2), 14. Love and peace (p.6), 15. Llama (p.6), 16. Fun activities (p.17), 17. Samba (p.8), 18. Into the mountain (p.12), 19. Endless snake/Sleeping dragon (p.16), 20. Great Wall (p.16), 21. Peru (p.6), 22. Pigeon (p.10), 23. Imaginary train (p.6), 24. Hot air balloon (p.12), 25. El Castillo (p.4), 26. Take a picture with her (p.6), 27. Twenty-two years (p.14), 28. Ciao (p.10), 29. Yoga (p.14), 30. Seven (p.4, 6, 8, 10, 12, 14, 16).

ADVENTURE SNAPSHOT PAGE

This section is all yours! Each page is waiting for a new adventure.
Fill them in, add photos, and make your own travel story.
And if you need more pages, just ask a grown-up to use the code and print more for you.

PRINT MORE PAGES HERE!

ADVENTURE SNAPSHOT PAGE

This is a sample of my "Day at the Beach" so you know how to fill out yours.

ALL ABOUT MY TRIP TO: Day at the Beach

When did you go?	Summer
Who went with you?	Family and friends
How old were you?	3
How did you get there?	By car
How long did it take to get there?	45 minutes

3 FUN THINGS YOU DID:

1 Built sand castles

2 Jumped over waves

3 Played frisbee

Best thing you ate: Ice cream

Coolest thing you saw: A dolphin

Favorite part of the trip:
Enjoying the sunset while laughing together

ADVENTURE SNAPSHOT PAGE

ALL ABOUT MY TRIP TO: _____

When did you go?	
Who went with you?	
How old were you?	
How did you get there?	
How long did it take to get there?	

3 FUN THINGS YOU DID:

1 _____

2 _____

3 _____

Favorite part of the trip:

_____

_____

_____

Best thing you ate: _____

Coolest thing you saw: _____

Place your favorite photo from this adventure.

ADVENTURE SNAPSHOT PAGE

ALL ABOUT MY TRIP TO: _____

When did you go?	
Who went with you?	
How old were you?	
How did you get there?	
How long did it take to get there?	

3 FUN THINGS YOU DID:

1 _____
_____

2 _____

3 _____

Favorite part of the trip:

_____

_____

_____

Best thing you ate: _____

Coolest thing you saw: _____

Place your favorite photo from this adventure.

ADVENTURE SNAPSHOT PAGE

ALL ABOUT MY TRIP TO: _____

When did you go?	
Who went with you?	
How old were you?	
How did you get there?	
How long did it take to get there?	

3 FUN THINGS YOU DID:

1 _____

2 _____

3 _____

Best thing you ate: _____

Coolest thing you saw: _____

Place your favorite photo from this adventure.

Favorite part of the trip:

_____

_____

_____

ADVENTURE SNAPSHOT PAGE

ALL ABOUT MY TRIP TO: _____

When did you go?	
Who went with you?	
How old were you?	
How did you get there?	
How long did it take to get there?	

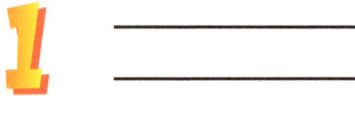

3 FUN THINGS YOU DID:

1 _____

2 _____

3 _____

Favorite part of the trip:

_____

_____

_____

Best thing you ate: _____

Coolest thing you saw: _____

Place your favorite photo from this adventure.

ADVENTURE SNAPSHOT PAGE

ALL ABOUT MY TRIP TO: _____

When did you go?	
Who went with you?	
How old were you?	
How did you get there?	
How long did it take to get there?	

3 FUN THINGS YOU DID:

1 _____

2 _____

3 _____

Favorite part of the trip:

_____

_____

_____

Best thing you ate: _____

Coolest thing you saw: _____

Place your favorite photo from this adventure.

ADVENTURE SNAPSHOT PAGE

ALL ABOUT MY TRIP TO: _____

When did you go?	
Who went with you?	
How old were you?	
How did you get there?	
How long did it take to get there?	

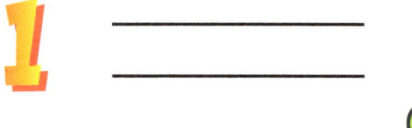

3 FUN THINGS YOU DID:

1 _____

2 _____

3 _____

Best thing you ate: _____

Coolest thing you saw: _____

Favorite part of the trip:

_____

_____

_____

Place your favorite photo from this adventure.

ADVENTURE SNAPSHOT PAGE

ALL ABOUT MY TRIP TO: _____

When did you go?	
Who went with you?	
How old were you?	
How did you get there?	
How long did it take to get there?	

3 FUN THINGS YOU DID:

 _____

 _____

3 _____

Best thing you ate: _____

Coolest thing you saw: _____

Place your favorite photo from this adventure.

Favorite part of the trip:

_____

_____

_____

ADVENTURE SNAPSHOT PAGE

ALL ABOUT MY TRIP TO: _____

When did you go?	
Who went with you?	
How old were you?	
How did you get there?	
How long did it take to get there?	

3 FUN THINGS YOU DID:

1 _____

2 _____

3 _____

Favorite part of the trip:

_____

_____

_____

Best thing you ate: _____

Coolest thing you saw: _____

Place your favorite photo from this adventure.

ADVENTURE SNAPSHOT PAGE

ALL ABOUT MY TRIP TO: _____

When did you go?	
Who went with you?	
How old were you?	
How did you get there?	
How long did it take to get there?	

3 FUN THINGS YOU DID:

1 _____

2 _____

3 _____

Best thing you ate: _____

Coolest thing you saw: _____

Place your favorite photo from this adventure.

Favorite part of the trip:

_____

_____

_____

ADVENTURE SNAPSHOT PAGE

ALL ABOUT MY TRIP TO: _____

When did you go?	
Who went with you?	
How old were you?	
How did you get there?	
How long did it take to get there?	

3 FUN THINGS YOU DID:

1 _____
_____

2 _____
_____

3 _____
_____

Best thing you ate: _____

Coolest thing you saw: _____

Favorite part of the trip:

_____
_____
_____

Place your favorite photo from this adventure.

ADVENTURE SNAPSHOT PAGE

ALL ABOUT MY TRIP TO: _____

When did you go?	
Who went with you?	
How old were you?	
How did you get there?	
How long did it take to get there?	

3 FUN THINGS YOU DID:

1 _____

2 _____

3 _____

Favorite part of the trip:

_____

_____

_____

Best thing you ate: _____

Coolest thing you saw: _____

Place your favorite photo from this adventure.

ADVENTURE SNAPSHOT PAGE

ALL ABOUT MY TRIP TO: _____

When did you go?	
Who went with you?	
How old were you?	
How did you get there?	
How long did it take to get there?	

3 FUN THINGS YOU DID:

1 _____

2 _____

3 _____

Favorite part of the trip:

_____

_____

_____

Best thing you ate: _____

Coolest thing you saw: _____

Place your favorite photo from this adventure.

ADVENTURE SNAPSHOT PAGE

ALL ABOUT MY TRIP TO: _____

When did you go?	
Who went with you?	
How old were you?	
How did you get there?	
How long did it take to get there?	

3 FUN THINGS YOU DID:

1 _____

2 _____

3 _____

Favorite part of the trip:

_____

_____

_____

Best thing you ate: _____

Coolest thing you saw: _____

Place your favorite photo from this adventure.

WORDS TO EXPLORE

Muchas gracias – "Thank you very much" in Spanish.
Olá – "Hello" in Portuguese.
Obrigado – "Thank you" in Portuguese.
Ciao – "Hello" or "Goodbye" in Italian.
Grazie – "Thank you" in Italian.
Marhaban – "Hello" in Arabic.
Namaste – "Hello" in Hindi, often said with hands pressed together.
Nihao – "Hello" in Chinese.

Adventure – A fun journey to discover new things.
Wonder of the World – A very special and amazing place.
Fascinating – So cool it grabs your attention.
Homeland – The country where you are from.
Maya – Ancient people who built great cities in Central America.
Remarkable – So special it makes you say "Wow!"
Ceviche – Raw fish in citrus juice, popular in Latin America.
Pan Flute – A wind instrument with pipes, used in Andean music.
Incas – Ancient people who built stone cities in South America.
Scenery – Beautiful views of nature.
Symbolizes – When something shows an idea, like a dove for peace.
Picanha – A tasty Brazilian cut of beef.

Carnaval Mask – A colorful mask worn during Carnival celebrations.

Samba – A lively dance from Brazil.

Gladiator – A brave fighter from ancient Rome.

Vespa – A stylish Italian scooter.

Gelato – Creamy Italian ice cream.

Continent – A large area of land on Earth.

Nabatean – Ancient people who built Petra in the desert.

Hummus – A creamy dip made from chickpeas.

Dates – Sweet fruit from date palm trees.

Temple – A place where people pray.

Magnificent – Very beautiful or amazing.

Ivory – A creamy white color.

Tuk Tuk – A small, three-wheeled vehicle.

Gulal – Bright powder used during Holi in India.

Dome – A roof shaped like half a ball.

Chinese Dragon – A long, snake-like creature from Chinese stories.

Dumplings – Dough filled with meat or vegetables.